GEORGE H. MCVEY

The Case
of the
Secret Admirer

Cindy Ryder, Girl Detective

Cindy Ryder Girl Detective:

The Case or the Secret Admirer

Join George's newsletter and receive a FREE copy of Grandpa Mac's Tall Tales. This is an exclusive short story collection you can only get by joining George H. McVey's newsletter. It isn't for sale anywhere. You can sign up at:
https://dl.bookfunnel.com/i2dowv4qmk.

Dedication

    This book is dedicated to Miss Jayna Sykes who asked her grandmother if I'd ever thought about writing a young teen book. The idea had been in the back of my mind and she helped me solidify it. So Jayna, I hope you enjoy being a character and that this book is the first of many adventures that you get to have not just in the pages of a book but in your real life as well.

    It's also dedicated to a young lady who aspires to be an author, Miss Katie Ciecalone. Her enthusiasm encouraged me to keep writing during a hard-fought struggle with my health. Thanks, Katie, I can't wait to see the stories you bring to the world.

    George

Table of Contents

One

Jayna Cody didn't know what to do. This was the third day in a row that she had arrived at the schoolhouse in Redemption, New Mexico, to find a gift sitting on her desk. None of the students were here yet and there was no one anywhere near the building who could be the person who had left them. The first day had been a poem written just for her. Or so the writer said in the note above the poem. Yesterday had been a bunch of wildflowers tied with a pretty pink hair ribbon. A note attached said the beauty of the flowers paled next to her own. Today was a book by her favorite author. This gift kind of disturbed her because it said whoever was leaving them knew her quite well.

None of the notes had the author's name; they had all been signed *Love, Your Admirer*. While it was flattering to think that someone thought her beautiful, worthy of a love poem, and paid enough attention to know who her favorite author was, it was also kinda scary, because they hadn't told her who they were. *How can I thank them for the gifts, or even know if they were someone I'd want to give me gifts if they don't tell me who they are? I mean I want to be courted; I'd love to have a beau and know someone might want to marry me someday. However, I expect to know who they are.*

She knew this couldn't be one of her students because the handwriting wasn't familiar. Plus, the book would have cost more than a child would have. She put the book with the things she had brought from home today. This was a mystery for after school; right now, she needed to get the floor swept and the fire going in the stove so the room would be clean and warm for her students when they arrived.

Still, as she went about her morning routine, she couldn't stop wondering who was sending her these gifts and their intention. She had signed an agreement with the school board that she would not keep company with any member of the opposite sex as long as she was employed as a teacher. This, to her way of thinking, was very old-fashioned and unfair. She'd never heard of a school board that asked a male teacher to be single or forsake courting while teaching. She'd mentioned that to her Uncle Nathan Ryder, and he agreed but the school board refused to change their rules.

She looked up at the sound of feet hurrying her way and saw her little brother; Levi, along with Cindy, David, and Nate Ryder all coming in the door. Cindy smiled at her and came up to the desk. "Hey, Cousin Jayna, we thought we'd come to see if you needed any help this morning. Pa gave us a ride in on his way to the Marshal's Office."

"Thank you, Cindy. You can help me by making sure everyone's desk is dusted and the seats wiped down. Boys, could you three go and bring in enough wood to fill the wood box for the day?"

"Okay, Sis."

Jayna sighed as she looked at the book on her desk and picked it up. "What's that, Cousin Jayna? Did you get a new book?"

"In a way I did, Cindy."

"What do you mean, in a way you did? Either you did or you didn't."

"I've been finding little gifts left on my desk this week; today it was this book."

Cindy smiled. "Do you have a secret beau none of us knows about? I'd have heard if Mama or Aunt Maryanne were talking about you having a beau."

Jayna shook her head. "No, that's the thing; I don't know who they're from. They're all signed *Love, Your Admirer.*"

"Oh, a secret admirer. That's romantic."

At thirteen Cindy was of the age where almost anything having to do with a boy was either disgusting or romantic. "I guess in a way it is." Jayna shook her head. "But it's creepy, too. How are they getting into the school when it's locked? These gifts say that whoever it is knows a lot about me. Are they watching me?"

"Sounds like you should talk to Pa and Uncle Bart about it."

"No, I don't think so; nothing that's been done is criminal. Well, maybe breaking into the schoolhouse but even that doesn't mean I need to get your father or mine involved."

Just then, the boys came back in with armloads of wood and students started arriving. It was time to put thoughts of her admirer out of her head and focus on teaching her students.

"Good morning, class."

The students responded as always, "Good morning, Miss Cody."

Then the day was begun.

Two

Cindy Ryder was curled up in the loft of the barn on her family's ranch, The Dueling N's. She was reading "The Adventures of Sherlock Holmes" by Sir Arthur Conan Doyle for the hundredth time. She knew she should be in the sewing room with her mother working on her embroidery or sewing, but she hated doing those things. She didn't know why everyone thought she should know how to sew and embroider, cook, or take care of babies. She wouldn't need any of those things to be a U.S. Marshal like Pa. And that was what she was going to be. Or a Pinkerton Detective like Kate Warne and Hattie Lawton. But everyone kept telling her women couldn't do those things. Didn't they realize that it was almost a new century? After all, in three short years it would be 1900 and it was time for the old ways of the 1800s to be put to rest. She didn't care what they said, she wanted to be a detective and marshal and she was going to prove them all wrong.

She'd already solved one case for her Aunt Hanna. It was weird calling Hanna aunt because she was younger than Cindy, but she was Grandfather David and Grandma's daughter so that made her Cindy's aunt. She'd told Pa that someone had taken her puppy, but Pa and all the other lawmen in town had told her it had probably just gotten lost. But Hanna was certain that someone had taken it. Cindy had promised to find it using deductive reasoning like Holmes and the tracking skills she'd learned by convincing Pa to take her when he went hunting. Sure enough, there were tracks of a person beside those of the puppy leading away from the house. She'd followed them and found the puppy along with the son of one of Grandpa David's sharecroppers. The puppy had been returned and Cindy, being the kind heart that she was, had gone to Grandpa Abner and gotten the little boy a puppy of his own.

She loved helping people and knew that she wanted to be a sheriff, marshal, or detective and knew she'd make a good one. She knew that while not widely accepted yet, there were female sheriffs; she had met a couple of them. She still remembered the first one. It was when her family had gone to visit friends of Pa's when she was five, almost six years old. She'd been surprised when she'd seen a woman wearing a sheriff's badge enter the restaurant where they were eating.

The woman caught sight of Pa and walked toward them. "Nathan Ryder, as I live and breathe. What brings you to my little town? Lookin' fer an outlaw I should know about?"

Pa had stood and smiled at the woman. "Calamity. No, nothing like that; came to talk to a man about some horses. Brought my family with me. Have you met my wife, Grace?"

The woman shook her head. "Ain't had the pleasure. Ever' time our paths have crossed you've been chasing some outlaw."

"Well, Grace Ryder, this is Miss Calamity Jane Canary. Calamity, my wife Grace."

"It's a pleasure to meet ya, ma'am, but it's Mrs. Burke now, Preacher. I got married since you been this way last."

Jane looked at Cindy and smiled. "And who is this young cowgirl princess?"

Cindy's eyes got big. "That's what Pa and Aunt Aggie call me. My name's Lucinda Elizabeth Ryder but everyone calls me Cindy. Is you the Sheriff?"

"I most certainly am, little lady."

"But you's a girl! Girls can't be sheriffs."

Calamity Jane laughed, "Well I am, so I reckon girls can be anything they set their minds to be. If they can find men willing to get outta the way and let 'em."

That was the day that five-year-old Cindy Ryder knew she was going to be just like her Pa. So she read Sherlock Holmes, she read all the dime novels about Nugget Nate and her Pa, and even the ones about her Uncle Bart. She'd met detectives and lawmen and if they'd talk to her, she'd talk with them. But most of all, she read True Detective Magazine, learning from the articles about how to be a better detective and the stories of how Pinkerton detectives solved some of the most difficult and exciting cases. She was going to work as a detective when she grew up, but she wasn't gonna wait to be all grown up to be one. There was a mystery right here in Redemption and she was gonna solve it. She'd find out who was leaving her cousin Jayna secret admirer gifts and prove she was already a detective.

She grabbed her composition book and pencil and started to make notes on what she already knew. Whoever it was had left notes, so they knew how to write. According to what Jayna had said, they had all been left at the school so they either had a key or access to a key, or they knew how to pick a lock. She'd have to look at the door lock tomorrow when she arrived at school to look for the tell-tale scratches that would be around the lock if it had been picked. Next, she wrote out some questions she'd need to ask Jayna in order to gather more information that would help her find the clues that would lead to the identity of Jayna's secret admirer.

Cindy got so caught up in making her notes and writing out questions that the day got away from her, and she was startled when the bell rang calling everyone in for supper. Her ma was adamant that the family be on time for dinner and washed up as well. Cindy put her pencil and composition book back into the school bag and hurried out of the hayloft to wash up for supper. She would be in enough trouble for skipping out of sewing time; she didn't want to add to it by being late and dirty, too.

Three

Jayna Cody climbed out of bed. Two more days and she could sleep in a little. She loved being Redemption's teacher, but she didn't like having to be up before dawn. Granted, if she'd married one of the farmers or ranchers around the area, she'd still be up before dawn, but a woman can dream of a rich banker, lawyer, or even a not-so-rich shopkeeper, can't she? One where she had a cook and a maid and could sleep until seven or eight in the morning. But not her, she was the schoolteacher, and with the rules the school board had put in place, she'd be an old maid and still alone teaching kids when she was twenty-five.

Not that she was really alone. Yes, she lived in this tiny cottage that Uncle Nathan had built for Jane Landry while she was the schoolteacher. Officially, it wasn't a perk of the job since Uncle Nathan wasn't on the school board, but Jane was the daughter of Pastor Peter from Cottonwood and Uncle Nathan wanted to take care of her. When she'd moved home to care for her sick friend's family, another teacher had filled in, but she had married last year and now Jayna was the new teacher.

She needed to go see her family tonight. Her little sister, Paulina, hadn't been at school yesterday, and Levi had told her that she was feeling sick. She knew Mama Maryanne could take care of Paulina, but Jayna felt worried. She'd helped take care of the child since she was a baby. She'd been right there when the doctor had delivered her and had helped Mama Maryanne and Papa Bart care for both Paulina and Levi since they adopted her. She needed to see for herself that her sister was okay.

She knew it was unfounded, but she'd been this way ever since her whole family had died of a fever. She was the only one to survive and the uncle that took her in wasn't a nice man. By the time he got himself killed in a bar fight, she was happy to go live at the orphanage. But she'd gotten a blessing in the Cody's and she loved them all just like she had been born a Cody. Tonight, she'd hitch up Beauty and go visit her family and see if there was anything she could do to help Mama with Paulina or any of her other chores.

Jayna had started to get ready for school when she noticed that her favorite combs were missing. Without them, she couldn't do her hair the way she wanted for school. She'd just have to do a simple bun and worry about where she'd misplaced her combs later. She couldn't understand where they would have gone; she'd taken them off when she came home yesterday and placed them in her jewelry box on her dressing table just like always. Now they were nowhere to be seen.

She left her little house and almost tripped on the package laying on her first step. From the handwriting, she knew without a doubt that it was another gift from her admirer. This time whoever it was had come to her home and not broken into the schoolhouse. She opened the package to see a note on top of two silver hair combs with beautiful jeweled butterflies on the tops of each comb. She stopped as she had a disturbing thought. How was it that these new beautiful combs showed up on her stoop the same time that her old combs from her mother disappeared? She opened the note and almost screamed. *Jayna my love, I noticed that your hair combs were looking a little worn for wear. I hope these new ones will please you, as I know it will please me to see you wearing them. Knowing that you are a creature of habit, I removed those old worn out things so you could try your new ones.*

Love,

Your Admirer

He had been in her house! This time she was going to take Cindy's advice and go right to her Papa Bart and Uncle Nathan. Whoever this person was, they'd broken into her house while she slept, came right into her room and removed her last remembrance of her mother. While it upset her to lose the combs that had been her mother's, it was more troublesome that someone had entered her room while she slept. They could have done anything! This time they'd gone beyond childish and done something very wrong. It was time to get her family involved. She ran down the boardwalk ignoring the greetings from the citizens of Redemption. She felt scared and unsafe for the first time since the Cody's adopted her; she needed to get to the Marshal's office and see Papa Bart and Uncle Nate.

Four

Cindy saw her teacher heading to the Marshal's office. "Pa, I think Jayna needs to talk to you and Uncle Bart. She's coming here in a hurry and she looks upset."

Nathan walked up beside her and looked up the street. "I wonder what has her in such a state."

Cindy noticed the piece of paper wadded in Jayna's hand and the box in her other one. "It looks like she got another gift from her secret admirer. Only this time, whatever she got seems to have upset her instead of being pleasant."

Both men looked at the younger girl - almost a woman - standing looking out the window. "What are you talking about, Cindy Ryder?"

Cindy turned and looked at the two marshals. "Someone has been leaving gifts for Jayna in the schoolhouse every morning. They've somehow gotten in, although the door was locked, and left her something along with a note signed *Love, Your Admirer*. She told me about them yesterday; she'd gotten three of them. I would say based on the note in her right hand and the box in her left that she got another one and that, whatever it is, it has her upset."

Just then, they heard Jayna's footfalls on the boardwalk in front of the office; the door flew open as the young woman stormed in. "Oh, thank God you're both here!"

She went straight to Bart and wrapped her arms around him. The older Marshal looked over her shoulder at Cindy's Pa and his face said he didn't know what to do. "What's the problem, princess? You're shaking something fierce."

Cindy listened as Jayna poured out the story of her admirer and the increasingly intimate and personal gifts she'd been getting every day that week. "Papa Bart, when I got ready for school this morning, I couldn't find my hair combs, the ones I still had from my mother. They weren't where I put them before I went to bed last night. When I went out to open the schoolhouse, this package was on my front stoop."

She handed the box and note to her father; Nathan and Cindy moved where they could see it. When they finished reading the note, the two men looked at each other. "I don't understand, Jayna. What is the problem? Don't you like the new combs?"

Jayna gasped and Cindy laughed. "You two don't understand what has her upset? Really? After all the outlaws you've caught and crimes you've solved, you don't realize her admirer was in her house last night while she was asleep?"

Both men looked at the thirteen-year-old girl. "What gives you that idea, Cindy?"

Cindy sighed. "He said so in that note you just read, didn't he? He removed Jayna's old combs so she'd use the new ones." She looked back and forth between the two men, realizing they still didn't understand. "Pa, to do that when she took them off and put them on her dressing table before going to bed means whoever wrote that note had to enter her house and her bedroom while she was asleep and take them."

Bart looked like he wanted to hunt down and shoot someone and Cindy's Pa looked shocked that he'd not thought of that. "Are you two saying someone unknown somehow slipped into Jayna's home and took those combs from her dressing table?"

"Not only did they take them, but they also had to do it while she was sleeping in the bed in that room, Pa."

Bart looked at his adopted daughter and Cindy knew what was coming next. "You'll stay at the ranch until we figure this out."

Cindy could tell that Jayna wanted to argue against it, but the thought of a stranger entering her bedroom while she slept had her very upset. "As a matter of fact, I'm going to go and tell everyone that school is canceled today. You don't need to be trying to teach the youngsters with this on your mind. You go with Cindy and get your things; we'll rent you a buggy to take you out to the house. You tell your mom and Grace what happened, and they'll help keep an eye out for anyone who might try to get on the Dueling N's that don't belong there."

"I want to help find this owl hoot, Uncle Bart. I know more about what he's sent Jayna than you and Pa do; you need me."

Nathan nodded at her. "You're right, Cindy; we do need you. We need you to go with your cousin. No one will mess with her on the way out to the ranch with you with her. Once you get home you can write out a detective report for me. Isn't that what you'd do if you were working with the Pinkertons on a case like this? Write a report for Allan to give to the local law to use to track the criminal?"

Cindy wanted to argue because she knew Pa had only said that to get her back on the ranch because he still saw her as his little girl. It didn't matter that she was almost a grown woman; in just a few short years she'd be as old as some of the married women in town were now. No, he'd used her love of the Pinkertons and the fact that a detective would write a report on this type of case and her Pa knew it as well. Because this was a local matter, Pinkerton would probably insist that a report be made to the local law officers who would then follow up on the report. Still, Cindy wanted to catch this person and figure out why they were acting so strange. If this person really liked Jayna Cody, why didn't he just come and ask for permission to court her?

Cindy would write the report, but she'd continue to keep her eyes open, too. Since she was going back to Jayna's to let her get some clothes, she'd look around while she was there. She'd show her Pa and the whole town she could be a detective and she'd do it by catching Jayna's creepy admirer.

Five

Jayna watched Cindy as they walked back to Jayna's home. The girl's eyes never stopped moving. Cindy had the awareness both Uncle Nathan and Jayna's own Pa had. She seemed to take in everything at a glance. The difference was that while the men in their family took those things in looking for a threat, Cindy seemed to be looking for something no one else could see. When they got to her little cabin behind the school, Jayna went straight in and packed a few days' worth of clothes and her school supplies. She looked out the window to see Cindy bent over and walking around the yard looking intently at the ground as she walked. The sight of the girl made Jayna giggle. Jayna knew her little adopted cousin wouldn't appreciate her finding Cindy's antics funny, she couldn't help watching the young almost-lady walk with her nose near the ground and, as Aggie Cutler would have put it, "her caboose in the air for all to see." When she was packed and saw the girl on her knees by the front door looking in the latch hole, she couldn't stand it any longer. "Cindy Ryder, what in the world are you doing?"

The younger woman looked up as if it should be obvious. "I'm looking for clues to who your admirer is and how he got into your place."

"You should leave that to your Pa and mine. They'll find him."

"No, they won't. You watch; they'll come over, walk around the place, look for signs of tracks that could indicate who it was and where they came from or went. Then they'll come inside, look for an open window, and ask if you pulled the latchstring inside. You'll tell them you did, and they'll tell you they didn't see any tracks or forced entry and that you should plan to come back to the ranch and stay till they catch whoever it is. But they'll be wrong."

Jayna frowned "What do you mean, they'll be wrong."

"I mean there are clues here, and in everything that's been done already, that lead to the identity of your admirer. I don't know who he is yet, but I do know several things already."

"You do? What do you know and how could you know it when you say our Pas won't know it?"

Cindy sighed as she sat in the rocker by the fireplace in the parlor. "Because Pa and Uncle Bart know how to track outlaws and desperados; your admirer is neither of those things. They aren't looking for the right clues, because they haven't been trained to be a detective."

Now Jayna did laugh. "I have news for you, Cindy. I know what you've been taught and neither have you."

Cindy glared at her cousin. "You're just like the rest of them. You hear me but you don't listen, and you don't understand what I'm saying."

"What are you talking about?"

"I'm not saying another word until Pa and Uncle Bart tell you what I said they would. I might not say anything then. It would serve you and them right for never listening to me."

Jayna opened her mouth to try and soothe her younger friend. She remembered when she'd come to the ranch, she wasn't much younger than Cindy was now and, except for Nathan's great-aunt Aggie, she hadn't felt like anyone had listened to her, either. Just as she was going to apologize, her Pa and uncle stepped into the cabin. Bart and Nathan looked around the house; sure enough, she heard them rattling at the windows making sure they were secure just like Cindy had said. Then they went outside and walked around and around the house in ever-widening circles before coming back in.

Her Papa Bart came to her and looked at the carpetbag she'd filled, "Go get the rest of your things packed, Jayna. You'll need to stay at the ranch until we figure out who was in here last night and how they got in. Until we know more about who has been doing this to you, it isn't safe for you to stay here by yourself."

Cindy huffed and Jayna's eyes widened as she realized her Papa Bart had said exactly what Cindy said he would. "Okay, Cindy, out with it; what did you see that our Pas didn't? You know something."

Cindy looked at them, "I know lots of things, but no one listens so why should I say anything?"

Jayna's Uncle Nathan looked down at his daughter. "Young lady, if you know something about all this, you'd better tell me now. This isn't one of your games or stories."

Cindy stood and stamped her foot. "I don't play games, Pa. I've told you I've been studying. I know lots about Jayna's admirer, and if you let me see that letter for myself, I'll know even more."

Nathan looked at his irate daughter. "You say you've been studying when you want to hole up in the barn and read dime novels instead of working on your needlework. Do you think your mama and I don't know that?"

"Well, you and mama are wrong. I ain't reading dime novels. I'm reading true crime stories, stories from the Pinkerton files magazine, and Sherlock Holmes. Learning how to be a detective. How to hone my skills at observing and deducing. Studying how to be a detective like I said I would be one day. And it's helped; I know lots of things by observing and deducing about Jayna's admirer, including how he got in the house last night."

Jayna could see that her Uncle Nathan was getting his Scotsman up, as Bulldog O'Malley called it, so she stepped in. "What do you know? Show us what you know and explain how you know it, Cindy. You want us to listen, understand, and believe you? Tell us what you've observed and deduced and show us you're right."

Cindy looked at her and nodded. "Fine, I know that your admirer is well off financially and therefore probably not one of the miners, farmers, or cowboys, and definitely not one of your students. Those combs cost money. They have real jewels in them and are made of silver and gold. That means someone who could afford to buy them, so none of the people I've just listed. They're educated. That's based on the fact that they wrote you a poem and knew to get you a book as a gift. An uneducated or undereducated person wouldn't think of a book as a gift and, if so, they would have just bought whatever was on hand at the mercantile, not ordered a book you were looking forward to reading. I haven't seen the letter that was with the gift today, but I know if I did, I could tell you if they were right- or left-handed."

Six

Jayna almost laughed as she saw the look of irritation that flashed on her Uncle Nathan's face. His daughter was all red-haired spitfire and had just challenged him to listen to her and give her a chance to prove her reading was more than fun by telling him she could provide the two Marshal's with clues to Jayna's secret admirer by reading the letter the admirer had left for Jayna the night before.

Nathan, almost as a challenge, reached in his pocket and handed it to her.

Cindy unfolded it and looked closely at it for a few minutes.

She held it close to her face as she read it, studying the paper and the writing. "Well, he is left-handed and very smart, not just educated but wise."

Nathan frowned, "How can you possibly know that from that short note?"

Cindy raised her head. "I know more than that from the note, those were just the things I learned that I hadn't already known."

"Cindy, that's not possible; it's a few short lines."

"Jayna, do you have some paper, a pen, and ink around here somewhere?"

Jayna smiled; she knew Cindy was being impertinent on purpose now because her father refused to see what was becoming obvious to Jayna. Cindy did know what she was talking about. She had been learning to observe and deduce. "You know I do; you little show off. I'm the schoolteacher after all."

Cindy grinned at her. "Will you get some so I can show my father what should be obvious?"

Jayna turned and grabbed the paper, pen, and inkwell, getting her face under control as she did. She sat them on the table.

Cindy looked at her father. "You can draw and shoot with both hands; can you write with them both, too?"

Nathan nodded. "Yes."

"Then, Pa, will you please write the following sentence with your left hand on the paper in front of you."

Nathan filled the pen and set it to paper as Cindy told him what to write. "I am writing this sentence to demonstrate once and for all my daughter Cindy's powers of deduction are indeed real."

He wrote the sentence and then laid the pen down. "So?"

"We aren't done yet. Now lay your left hand under that sentence making sure not to touch the ink and take the pen in your right hand and write the same sentence again."

When he was finished, he set the pen aside and looked at Cindy. "Well?"

"Well what? I would think if you compare the two, the difference would be obvious."

Jayna and her Papa Bart joined Nathan at the table. It only took a moment before Jayna saw what Cindy was talking about. "The left-handed script leans. Is that what you mean, Cindy?"

The girl nodded. "That's one of the things, yes."

Nathan grunted. "Could be he's faking being left-handed. Knew about the lean like you did, Cindy."

Cindy smiled. "Well if that were true, it would prove he was wise which is something else I said this letter does. But he is left-handed. Try and fake that left-hand lean with your right hand, Pa."

Nathan did as Cindy asked and even Jayna could see the difference after only a few words. "I see what you mean. It's not the same."

"No, but more telling than that, look at how the sentence written with your left hand is a bit smudged toward the right side of the words. You won't see that on either of the sentences written with your right hand, even the fake left-hand writing."

"What caused that?"

Cindy smiled. "Look at your left sleeve cuff, Pa. You'll see ink on it. Your cuff made it as it dragged over the wet ink from word to word."

They all looked up at the younger girl as if seeing her for the first time. "That is amazing, Cindy." Her father asked, "How does his letter tell you he's wise as well as smart?"

"It tells me more than that; it confirms he's financially well off, too. Look at the ink smudges where his cuff dragged; they are perfectly black. They were made by true India ink. Look at yours; they're kind of brownish because they were made with cheaper iron ink. He's wise because he thought to disguise his wealth in the note. He bought paper anyone around here would buy, from students to anyone writing a letter. Anyone, that is, except someone like him. People who buy India ink also buy high-quality stationery. But to do that would give him away. He didn't think about the ink because, like most people, ink is ink. Yet he did think about the paper. From this note, I know beyond a doubt the admirer is also a man; the handwriting is masculine, not like Jayna's or Mama's or Maryanne's would be. He's younger; no tremor like Grandma's, or Grandma G's, or even Granddaddy's would have."

"That still doesn't mean you know how he got in the house."

"No, it doesn't, but the same skills of observation and deduction do prove how he got in. He came in through the door."

"He couldn't have come through the door unless the latch string was out."

"He used the latch string and came through the door."

Both Jayna's Papa Bart and Uncle Nathan looked at her. "You left the latch string out?"

Before Jayna could indicate she hadn't, Cindy got offended. "How could you ask her that? You know she didn't; every Ryder female and Aunt Maryanne and Jayna have had it drilled into their heads by Aunt Aggie that you pull in the latchstring. She pulled it in, but he still used it to get in and that's how I know he lives with a woman, his mother, sister, or aunt."

Nathan stood, "Cindy Ryder, if you can prove both those statements, I will tell your mother to never make you sew again."

Cindy smiled and looked at Jayna and her Pa. "You both heard him; I call you to witness that mountain promise."

They all knew the sacred thing to the Ryder family that a mountain promise was. It was unbreakable and had to be witnessed to be binding. They both had been around the Ryders long enough to know the end to the ritual, "I bear witness."

Cindy giggled, "No more sore fingers."

Nathan stopped her. "Not yet, young lady. Prove both statements."

"I will, Pa, but first will you go and observe the outside of the door, particularly where the latch string comes out the hole in the door?"

Nathan walked over as Cindy pulled the latchstring in slowly. Nathan looked, "What am I looking for?"

"Do you see those deep, dark-colored scratches around and in the hole?"

"Yes."

"Take the tip of your knife and scrape out some of the dark color."

Her father did as she asked. "What am I looking at?"

"Touch, smell, and taste it. It's bootblack."

Nathan looked at her and did what she asked. "It is bootblack. How did you know?" "Because it's how I knew he lived with a woman. He used a shoe buttonhook to pull the string back out. The scratches gave me the initial thought and the shoe black confirmed it." She turned to Jayna, "Can I borrow your buttonhook a moment so I can demonstrate."

Jayna went back to her carpetbag and pulled out her buttonhook. "Here you go."

"Thank you. When me and Pa get outside, shut the door like you did last night before you went to bed."

Jayna nodded and pulled the door shut, dropped the latch in the catch, and pulled in the string letting it dangle.

Just when Jayna thought Cindy was not even going to try, the buttonhook slipped through the hole and snagged the string, then it was slowly drawn back through the hole and the latch bar was lifted and the door opened slowly and noiselessly. Nathan stood looking at the door and examined the hole. "You didn't leave any scratches; why did he?"

"I wasn't trying to open it in the middle of the night without a light to see by."

"Well okay, you've proved he used a buttonhook, but he could have bought one."

Cindy sighed. "Then there would have been scratches but no bootblack. Only a hook used by a woman on a Sunday would have bootblack on it, Pa."

Jayna laughed. "Well, Cindy, you have certainly proven your point and we hold your Pa to his mountain promise."

Jayna's Papa Bart laughed as well. "Maybe we should make her a deputy and bring her on all our adventures."

Nathan shook his head. "No, but I will certainly keep my promise, and more than that, I'll start buying those crime novels and Pinkerton stories for her myself if she's learning that much from them. We may not know yet who is doing this, but the suspect field just got smaller."

Bart nodded. "And with a few simple modifications, we can keep this from happening again. But until then, Jayna, come stay with your mama, brother, sister, and me."

Jayna nodded, "For a few nights, Papa Bart, until Paulina is better. I was going to come out anyway."

With that, they closed up the cabin and headed for the Dueling N's with Jayna feeling loved and safe, and she was sure her cousin felt vindicated. Jayna thought about it and realized that her little cousin might indeed become a female Pinkerton when she grew up. She certainly had impressive powers of observation and deduction. Who knew, maybe she would figure out who was leaving Jayna these gifts, but would that help her know what to do about him once she knew who he was? No, that was all on her.

Seven

Cindy rode out to the ranch with her cousin in the buggy that her father had rented for them. Her mind kept running over the case. She was missing something; she knew she was missing something. She couldn't figure out what she was missing but she knew she was missing an important clue. The more she thought about it the harder it was to figure out what she could be missing. She thought back to some of the things she'd read in the Pinkerton Files magazine. That one was her favorite because it didn't just tell about the cases, but the writer would often interview the detectives and ask them questions about how they came to their conclusions.

The magazine also had articles on learning to use deductive reasoning and observation. On how to question people to get them to tell you things they didn't want to tell. Other helpful hints and tips to becoming a detective. So, what was she missing? She thought of an article she had read the other day that said sometimes the best way to see what was hiding in plain sight was to distract yourself to stop thinking about it. That's what she needed to do. She needed to talk to Jayna about anything besides the case and think of something else for a while. Maybe her brain would click on what she was missing if she wasn't trying to get it to think about what she was missing.

"Were you really planning on coming out to the ranch for a few days before Uncle Bart said you had to?"

Jayna nodded. "Yes, you know how I am when someone I love gets sick; I can't help but worry. Hearing Paulina is sick worried me, so I had planned to come out after school and help Mama Maryanne until Paulina was feeling better."

Jayna pushed her hair out of her face; a few pieces had come loose from her bun. That's what did it; watching her cousin move her hair reminded her of a conversation she'd heard Jayna having Sunday with Cora Gunderson. "Hey, your hair combs that got taken. They were tin, right?'

"Yes, and old and starting to lose pieces."

"I remember you said Sunday that the silver plate was starting to come off and some of the jewels were falling out."

"Yes, I had put them in my jewelry box so I didn't lose them till I could get some more glue to paste them back in."

Cindy tried to remember if she'd looked in the jewelry box. "Do you remember if the jewels were still there this morning?"

Jayna shook her head. "I don't remember, but no one would take them, Cindy. They weren't real; they were just cut glass. They aren't worth anything."

Cindy thought about that and shook her head. "That's not true; they're worth something to you."

Jayna looked at her funny. "Yes, but only because they came from my mama's hair combs and they remind me of the good times before she died."

Cindy pulled her little notebook and a pencil out of her bag. She started making notes about things that she was thinking. "Let's play a game of pretend. I know you're the teacher but think with me. This person admires you, yes?"

Jayna shrugged. "That's what the note says."

"So, let's assume it's a man. We already know he's smart, wise, somewhat wealthy, and left-handed. Let's also pretend that he doesn't just admire you, but he fancies you. I mean he's trying to get your attention."

Jayna nodded. "I suppose that's true."

"I bet if we were to go back to your house and look, not one of the jewels from your hair combs are in the jewelry box. I think he took them all."

Jayna frowned "Why would he do that? He wanted me to wear his new expensive hair combs, that's why he took mine."

"I don't think that's why he took them. He said in his note he knew you wouldn't wear his if you had yours because you're a creature of habit. Right?"

"Yes."

"That means he's someone who knows you really well; that helps us narrow our search, too. He can't be a newcomer."

"Because he's watched me long enough to know my habits."

Cindy smiled. "Exactly. By Jove, Watson, I think you have it."

Jayna laughed at her almost-cousin's very bad English accent. "But why do you think that means he took my missing combs and the jewels?"

Cindy smiled. "Because he knows how important they are to you, and he knows why. I think he was at church on Sunday and heard your conversation with Cora. I think he took them to have them repaired for you. But he also wanted to give you something from himself to wear."

"So, if you're right, then I should get them back and the jewels will be pasted back in them."

Cindy nodded. "If I'm right. Now the question is would he be handy enough to fix it himself or would he take it to someone to fix for him?"

"What do you think?"

"I think he's in love with you or thinks he's in love with you."

Jayna blushed. "Okay."

"A man in love wants to impress the woman of his affection. I'm thinking he took them to someone to fix. An expert."

Jayna frowned. "They are at best costume jewelry. Who's an expert on costume jewelry?"

"Jeweler, watchmaker, tinker maybe."

"I don't think a jeweler would waste their time on them."

Cindy shook her head. "Never discount without reason. That's another thing I read about being a detective. Until I know he didn't take them to a jeweler, I have to think he might have. If he paid enough, a jeweler might have repaired them. Especially if your admirer told him they held sentimental value to the owner."

Jayna pulled into the ranch, and Cindy saw Jayna risk a look at Cindy. "You really are studying. You aren't just playing at being a detective, are you? You honestly want to be a detective."

Cindy smiled, finally someone was listening. She raised her arms in the air and in frustration let them fall back into her lap. "That's what I've been saying."

Jayna patted Cindy on the knee. "I know, but like everyone else, I thought you were just playing games. I'm sorry. From now on, you can come and talk to me about this dream and what you're learning anytime, Cindy. I'll do everything I can to try and help you prepare for your dream."

Cindy smiled. She wanted to hug her shy cousin, but she knew even if they weren't driving Jayna wouldn't like that. "Thank you. I might take you up on that when I get stuck or need help understanding what I'm reading."

Jayna smiled. "You know what, I bet you figure out who it is before my Papa Bart or your Pa does."

Cindy beamed. "I bet I do, too." She looked up. "Mama's outside hanging clothes. She's going to want to know why we're home."

"We tell her the truth. Then I'm going to go check on Paulina. You need to go make your report. Can I see what you do when you're done? We can consider it a writing assignment," Jayna said. "That way your mom will let you go work on it."

Cindy nodded. "Yeah, when I get it written up. I'm going to make a list, too. Of suspects just for you and me. As I get more information and eliminate or discover more clues, we should be able to narrow the list. That information is just for you. After all, you're my real client. Not Pa or Uncle Bart. You need to know who is leaving you those gifts. After I find him for you, if you decide you want them to stop, you can tell our Pas who it is."

Jayna looked at her with a frown. "What do you mean, if I want him to stop?"

Cindy sighed. "I know you want a beau, Jayna. Maybe you'll find one."

With that, they pulled to a stop. It was time to face her Mama Maryanne and tell her what was going on.

Just as Cindy said, both Grace and Maryanne wanted to know why school had been canceled. Once they explained, and Cindy told her mother she had an extra writing assignment to do for Jayna, the women all headed their separate ways. Grace and Cindy went over to the main ranch house, and Jayna and Maryanne to the foreman's house. Jayna went to check on Paulina and set her mind at ease that her sister was going to get well.

Eight

Jayna watched as Cindy went inside to use her Pa's office to work on her report. Jayna was amazed she'd just seen a very different side to the young woman. Maybe they all still saw the little girl playing Cowgirl Princess because that's what they were used to seeing. But this day had been eye-opening for Jayna as a teacher. Cindy had a dream; one she was working toward making a reality even when no one else had supported her. As Cindy's teacher, what if Jayna encouraged that dream? Helped Cindy with assignments tailored to help her achieve it. Like this report as her writing assignment. Or using one of her magazine articles as her reading assignment and having Cindy write a report on what she learned, helping her reinforce the information in the younger woman's mind. By doing so, she would be letting Cindy know someone in her life was listening and encouraging her to chase her dreams.

Was that something she could do with each of her students? It certainly wasn't school like she'd been taught to teach it. But wouldn't it connect her students and make them eager to learn? She'd have to give that a thought.

The other thing that she couldn't get out of her mind as she checked on her little sister was Cindy's declaration that she knew Jayna wanted a beau. But that wasn't really true; Jayna wanted what the Cody's had. She wanted a love that lasted. She'd heard their story, how Papa Bart's brother tricked him into running west leaving his new wife behind. How Mama had waited for six years to hear from him and then come west, presenting him with the son he never knew he had. How through all that time she never gave up on him, and he never stopped loving her. That's what she wanted; a love like that. But at the same time to find it now and have to decide if she'd pursue a chance or give up her job. Did she want to know who was giving her these gifts? Yes. Would she let it continue, knowing if the school board found out it would mean the end of her job? That she couldn't say.

What she could say was it was time for her to start seriously thinking about her own future. She didn't want to end up an old maid because she was the local schoolteacher. It was time for her to talk to local leaders again and see if the antiquated rules for being a schoolteacher could be changed. Maybe it was time she talked to someone who could give her some idea how to handle this whole mess. Not just the secret admirer mess, but her desire to find a suitor and become a wife along with her desire to keep teaching the children here in Redemption. Once she saw that Mama was resting and Paulina was indeed getting better, she headed over to the ranch house. If anyone could help her, it would be her friend and mentor Grace Ryder.

Jayna entered and headed up the stairs after learning from Mister Stillman that Grace was upstairs in her parlor. She climbed the stairs and stopped just outside the door, knocking on the frame to catch Grace's attention. The older woman looked up at her and smiled. "Jayna, come in and sit a spell. Would you like a cup of tea? Stillman just had some sent up."

Jayna poured herself a cup and settled into the chair across from her adopted aunt. Grace smiled at her. "Having someone invade your home while you were sleeping must have been frightening."

Jayna nodded. "It was, especially to wake and know that some man had been in my room while I was lying there asleep. It instantly reminded me of my past before I went to the orphanage. But I don't think he meant to hurt me or frighten me. I think he just didn't think about the danger or fright it would give me."

The older woman frowned. "Jayna, don't take this too lightly. I know your father and Nathan are worried. They wouldn't be if this wasn't serious."

"Oh, I'm not saying that whoever he is didn't do something wrong. Not knowing his identity is indeed worrisome. But at the same time, until he came into my house, I will admit that I was flattered by his gifts. He seems to know me quite well."

Grace smiled at her. "Yes, it is nice to have someone pay attention to you, isn't it? Even the not knowing who he is would be kind of exciting."

Jayna nodded "Exactly, and that brings me to why I came to see you. In a way what this secret admirer is doing is a type of twisted courtship." She held up her hand before Grace could caution her again. "I know it isn't the right way to go about courting me, and when we find out who he is I plan to make that plain to him. However, it did get me thinking and worrying about something else."

Grace sipped her tea and then leaned forward. "What did it get you thinking and worrying about?"

Jayna sighed. "I'm not getting any younger, Aunt Grace. Yet, because of the rules the school board has in place, I must either give up my job or remain unmarried and uncourted. Technically, if they wanted, I could be dismissed for what has already happened. I've received several gifts from a male who is not a relative. He was even in my home alone with me for a period of time. These are violations of those supposed morality rules."

Grace nodded. "Yes, I suppose they are. Why are you worried about this?"

Jayna tilted her head to the side. "Not really worried, just upset. This whole thing got me thinking about finding a suitor or being courted and drove home the fact that I can't do either. I can't take the first step to finding a love like you and Nathan or Mama Maryanne and Papa Bart have because of my position. Yet if I wanted to be courted or find a husband, I'd have to stop doing something else that I love, helping children discover their potential and teaching them. It isn't right, and it isn't fair. If the schoolteacher were a man, they wouldn't have these rules about courting. Nowhere in the country are those morality rules enforced on male teachers, just us females."

Grace nodded. "That is true. I came here originally to teach school, as you know. However, because I married Nathan before we got here the school board wouldn't allow me to teach. Of course, I was pregnant with Cindy by the time we arrived; but still you're right. If I'd been a man, being married wouldn't have stopped me from teaching."

Jayna stood and started to pace as she got irritated. "This is almost a new century, Aunt Grace. We women have the right to vote now. In other places these rules are being changed to at least allow a female teacher to court and marry. Yes, I can see how having an infant may be a reason not to teach. But what about after a woman's children are all school-age? Why can't she return to the classroom?"

"These are all good points Jayna. What do you want from me?"

"I want you to help me convince Uncle Nathan that we need to get the board to remove the courtship restrictions from my contract. I want to find a husband who loves me, and I want to be able to keep my position while courting him."

Grace nodded. "Very reasonable requests. I know Nathan will agree, but it isn't me or Nathan that we have to convince."

Jayna huffed out a frustrated breath. "No, we have to convince a bunch of men who have no vision to see that times have changed. They won't even consider it if I'm the one who brings it up. In fact, they may just terminate my contract if I do."

Grace looked thoughtful. "Let me talk to Nathan and some others. I'll help you with this, Jayna, because I agree with you. If you were a male teacher, it wouldn't even be an issue. We got the women to support us when we needed to convince the men to vote to give us a voice in government. So now I just need to convince them to support us in making these rules fair and open the door for you to be courted and marry without giving up what you feel is your calling."

Jayna went over and hugged her friend. "Thank you! I was hoping you would help me."

The older woman hugged her back. "Of course, I'll help you, Jayna. We all love you, and you've been a very good teacher. It would be a shame to lose you because you want a normal life with a husband and children. We will do our best to change the school board's mind."

After that, the conversation turned to the school itself and how the Ryder children were doing in class. Later, when Jayna finally left, she was feeling less burdened by the whole thing and hopeful that Grace could help her convince the school board to allow her to be courted when the time came.

Nine

Cindy sat looking over the report she had written for her pa. She'd detailed everything she knew and all the facts of the case up until now. She'd made sure to include her deductions and why she'd come to the conclusions she had. She felt that the case was laid out and the information was concise and well-articulated. She just hoped he'd actually consider the things she'd written. At least her demonstration at Jayna's cottage had shown him that she wasn't just playing games, and she'd won the freedom from the dreaded afternoon sewing and embroidery lessons she hated.

She laid aside the report for her pa and then put all the new clues she'd discovered into her composition book. Then she started to jot down what she needed to do to gather more clues and evidence of who might be Jayna's admirer. She kept coming back to the hair combs the man had taken. From what she could deduce, he knew Jayna; after all, he knew her love of poetry, gave her the gift of her favorite flowers tied with her favorite color of hair ribbon, and the newest book by her favorite author. It only made sense that he would know how special those combs were to her. So why did he take them?

That thought led her to the fact that several of the paste jewels from the combs were still in the jewelry box where Jayna kept them. They were in need of repair. Could he have taken them to have them repaired and refurbished? If so, then they would be returned in better condition than when he'd snatched them. Who would he take them to for repair? A tinker? Probably not, but maybe to the new jeweler in town. He dealt in both fine jewels and 'imitation jewelry' as he called it. Might those combs have been taken to him? If they had, how could she find out who had taken them there? Which led her to another thought: Who was Jayna's admirer?

She looked back over the clues she'd gathered and pulled another sheet of paper out of her Pa's desk. She listed all the single men that she knew either fit or came close to the deductions she made. The list was about fourteen names long. Then she went through her clues again and started crossing off each person that didn't fit the clues she had. The first four lived alone so they wouldn't have a woman's button hook to grab the cord with. Then two more were crossed out because she knew they were right-handed and the left-handed script was too neat and precise to be made by someone who was writing with their weaker hand as her pa had. That left her with eight. Three of those lived too far out of town to make the trip several times a week. She was left with five suspects. Just five. So now she knew who to keep an eye on. With Sunday services coming up soon she would see which one was paying close attention to her cousin Jayna. But before then, she'd try to get Levi to go into Redemption with her to visit the jeweler. Maybe they could find out if anyone brought him a set of combs to fix and if so, who it was.

She didn't want to involve her father or Uncle Bart because they would then want to arrest the culprit for breaking into Jayna's house. One of the men she thought might be the secret admirer had some history with the Cody's and Bart would want to throw him under the jail. Cindy thought holding something he'd done fourteen years ago when he was little more than a boy was ridiculous, but she knew how her pa and uncle thought. While they may be willing to forgive, as lawmen they couldn't forget.

Still, if he turned out to be Jayna's admirer, what would Uncle Bart do? More importantly, what would Jayna do? Cindy knew her friend and sort-of-cousin wanted to find love and marriage. At the same time, Jayna wanted to keep teaching school as well. As much as Cindy would hate to see Jayna leave the Redemption school, she deserved to be loved. Cindy tucked her list into her composition book and took the pages of her report. She'd use that as her excuse to go into town and see Pa. While there she'd swing in to see the jeweler, one of her other suspects for Jayna's secret admirer. Mister Cole Bryant was a dapper Bostonian and not at all who she thought her horse-loving cousin would be interested in but the one mystery that still eluded almost all detectives was what caused a couple to fall in love. It was funny, though, because matchmakers seemed to have it all figured out.

Cindy and Levi rode toward Redemption. Her mother had looked over the report she had made for Pa and agreed that she should take it to him. She praised Cindy for her penmanship and told her that if she was going to spend time learning to be a detective, it was a good thing her penmanship was so excellent. Cindy wanted to roll her eyes but knew that her mother would see it even if she didn't say anything. She loved her mother but for all her acceptance of the western lifestyle, she was still very much the southern belle she grew up being, and disrespect wasn't tolerated. Cindy, being smart, deduced it was wise to keep her thoughts on the subject of penmanship to herself lest she find herself once again having to sew and do embroidery.

Levi Cody looked over at her and asked, "Why are you really going to town Cindy?"

"You heard what I told our ma's; I'm taking my report to our pa's so they have the information they need to figure out who was in Jayna's house the other night."

The seventeen-year-old laughed. "I heard what you told them, but I know you, Cindy; there's something else you want to do in Redemption. Otherwise, you would have just waited until they got home tonight to give them that report. So, what are we really doing while we're in town?"

Cindy looked at the boy, suddenly a man, who lived on her ranch. She would never admit it to anyone, but she thought he was the most handsome cowboy working for her father. She was a little sad because she knew that soon he would be leaving. When this school year was over, Levi was heading east to go to university. She hated change and losing one of the only people who had always believed she would become a Lady Pink was hard for her.

She just knew when he finally came back to Redemption, if he came back, he'd have a wife. There was no way someone as good looking as Levi wouldn't end up married. She stiffened her resolve for when that happened. She'd hate it because he'd always been in her heart. However, when the time was right, she'd find a Pinkerton office, apply, and become a great detective. She didn't need to be sad about the boy next door finding happiness in the arms of another. "You always did know when I had a scheme planned, Levi."

He smiled and her heart, despite her recently resolved indifference, raced just a little at his handsome face. "Yes, Cindy, and I know that seeing our pas was just the excuse to get to town again. So, what are we really doing while we're there?"

Cindy went on to explain her theory about Jayna's secret admirer and her stolen hair combs. Levi listened and nodded. "That sounds feasible, and you want to see if Mister Bryant is repairing them?"

Cindy nodded. "Sort of. He is also one of the suspects on my list."

Levi slowed his horse and Cindy did the same. "You think Cole Bryant is Jayna's secret admirer?"

Cindy nodded "He could be, he fits all the clues. He's single, close to her age, lives with his mother, and is left-handed. He's also intelligent and makes enough money to afford real ink. So yes, he is one of the men I think could be her admirer. I want to talk to him either way. If he has the combs maybe he'll tell us who brought them to him if he didn't do it himself. If he did it himself, I'll be able to tell."

Levi looked at her with a smirk on his face. "You are a wonder, Cindy. One of these days they are going to be writing dime novels about you instead of Nugget Nate and The Preacher."

Cindy felt her cheeks heat up with the blush that was there. She hated that her coloring and red hair made her blush so easy. Yet she loved that it was Levi who could make her blush the most. "I don't care if they write stories about me. One day I just want to be the best female detective the Pinkertons have ever had."

"You will, of that I have no doubt. Now enough jaw waggin'. I'll race you to the town line."

Without another word, Cindy kicked her little mustang into a full gallop and laughed at catching her partner in her adventure unaware as they raced to town.

Ten

Cindy pulled up in front of the U.S. Marshal's office just a half-horse length ahead of Levi and laughed at her friend as he accused her of cheating. "All's fair in horse racing and gun fights, Levi, you know that."

He shook his head as he dismounted and then knocked her Lady Stetson down over her eyes. "One of these days, Cindy Ryder, I'll beat you fair and square."

"Keep trying, Levi, but it won't be anytime soon that you'll outsmart or outride me."

They were still laughing as they entered the marshal's office. Cindy looked up at Pa's smiling face. "We were wondering who came tearing up the street like a herd of buffalo; should have known it was you and Levi. What are you doing in town, Cindy?"

Cindy held the copy of her report out to Pa. "You asked me for this report, Marshal Ryder. I showed it to Ma who gave me high praise for my penmanship and told me I could bring it to you as long as Levi came with me."

Her father looked over each page and handed them off to Bart. "This is a very detailed and well-written report with all your thoughts and clues laid out. Well done, but I don't see a list of possible suspects and I know you have one, Cindy. Where are they?"

Cindy smiled at Pa. "You, Marshal Ryder, are not my client. Jayna is my client and I will give her the list of possible suspects if she asks. But at this time the list is too long, and I need more information and clues to narrow it down. I would not like to accuse the wrong person of being Jayna's admirer, especially since I know that you and Uncle Bart plan to go and try to arrest whoever it is."

"I could demand you tell me."

"Then, Marshal Ryder, I would again remind you that you are not my client. You are free to talk to my client and if she wishes to give you the results of my investigation when it is finished, that is between you and her. I cannot give you anything she hasn't authorized me to give to you."

Cindy could tell by the look on his face that Pa was not pleased with her answer. "You sure talk like one of those Pinkerton Detectives, that's for sure. Just remember, Cindy, that you aren't yet one of them. Allan Pinkerton can't protect you from your Pa."

Cindy bit her lip. "That's true, Pa. However, you and Ma are the ones who taught me to follow my principles and act with integrity. I haven't solved this case yet, but even when I do, I'll inform my client of her admirer's identity. If she wishes to share it with you, that's her right. Even if you punish me for it, I won't break my principles; I'll take the punishment."

He shook his head and sighed. "I won't punish you for not telling me, Cindy. I'm not happy, but if you are truly going to keep acting and taking cases as a detective, I won't force you to give me information. However, if I find out that you have information on a crime before, or right after, it happens and don't give that to the local law, I will rethink allowing you to take on cases. Is that understood?"

She nodded her head. "Yes, sir."

Not long after that, she and Levi were riding up the street to visit the jeweler.

Once they entered the store, Cindy saw Jayna's combs on Mister Bryant's workbench. They had been recoated with silver, and it looked like he was in the process of pasting the fake jewels back onto the top of the combs. He looked up and smiled. "Levi, Cindy, to what do I owe the honor of your patronage today? Have you come to pick up a gift for one of your mothers?"

Cindy stepped forward. "No, Mister Bryant. I'm actually working on solving a mystery. My cousin Jayna has asked me to help her figure out who the secret admirer is that keeps leaving her gifts. My clues so far have brought me to your shop to ask you a few questions. Have you sold a set of gold hair combs to one of these five people this week?" She handed him her list of suspects. "However, my second question was if that same person had given you a set of silver-plated combs to repair. I see the combs on your workbench, so I know the answer to my questions. You wouldn't be willing to tell me who brought you those combs to fix, would you?"

He smiled at her. "I could tell you who brought me those combs and who bought the gold ones I sold this week, but I don't talk about my clients to other people. You know that, Cindy. I wouldn't want to ruin someone's surprise gift to anyone."

"Was it one of the people on my list? Would you be willing to tell me that?"

The jeweler laughed. "No, I don't think I will answer that question, Cindy, but I will tell you that I'm impressed by your skills as an investigator. I am willing to tell you that the silver-plated combs I'm repairing will be ready for my customer to pick up on Saturday morning, just like I told them they would."

Cindy reached out and took her list of suspects back. "Thank you, Mister Bryant, you've been very helpful."

The shopkeeper laughed and shook his head. "Oh no I haven't young lady! I'm positive that I've not been helpful at all."

Cindy smiled and motioned for Levi to come with her as she left the store. "Well, you didn't find out anything there, Cindy. Why did you tell Cole he was helpful?"

Cindy looked at Levi and laughed. "You're a lot like Pa and your pa, Levi. Cole was helpful. He eliminated himself as one of my choices; he isn't Jayna's admirer. While he didn't tell me who it was, he gave me enough information that I know he did sell the gold combs to one of my suspects, and I'll have this case solved by Saturday."

"Who do you think it is?"

Cindy climbed on her mustang and the two of them headed back to the ranch. She told Levi that she couldn't tell him, but she did think she knew who Jayna's admirer was. Once they returned to the ranch, she went straight to the Cody's house and gave her report and list of suspects to Jayna. She informed her teacher she would have the case solved by Saturday morning. Surprised, the schoolteacher asked if Cindy had a main suspect from the four names left on the list of possible admirers she'd just given Jayna.

Cindy nodded and pointed to a single name on the list and told Jayna she'd know for sure by Saturday. Jayna hugged her student and friend. "Let me know when you've solved it for certain."

"I will. If I'm right, what are you going to do about it? I do know that you should get your mother's hair combs back on Monday. I suspect you'll find them on your desk at the schoolhouse when you show up Monday."

Jayna looked at her student. "What I do about it will depend a lot on what the school board decides after your mother talks to them this week. She and I are trying to get the rules changed so I can court and marry without losing my job right away. I will say, if you are right, I'm not opposed to courting that gentleman. He is quite handsome and kind."

Cindy agreed, and soon enough the two of them went on to talk about other things before Cindy went home to help Ma with chores around the house.

Saturday morning saw Cindy and Jayna sitting in Mahala's Restaurant having breakfast and talking about the week. Jayna spent most of her time talking to the parents who stopped in when they saw her to ask about school reopening. She informed them that since her own sister was well and no new cases of students coming down with the sickness had been reported, they would be back to school on Monday.

Cindy, on the other hand, kept her eyes on the jeweler's shop. Sure enough, about halfway through the morning, one of her suspects rode up and dismounted in front of the shop. Cindy pointed it out to Jayna, and they both watched as just a few minutes later he exited the shop with a brown paper wrapped package the perfect size to be Jayna's old hair combs. "I think that successfully solves your case, Miss Cody."

Jayna nodded. "I believe it does, Miss Ryder. You are a remarkable detective, Cindy Ryder, and I can't wait to see what you do in the years to come."

"Thank you, Jayna. I can't wait to become a Lady Pink, and I won't give up until I achieve my goal. What are you going to do about your admirer, now that you know who he is?"

Jayna smiled. "Well, since your mother informed me last night that the school board has agreed to change the rules and allow female teachers to court with proper chaperones and marry without losing their positions, I will invite him to dinner tomorrow night if he's in church in the morning.

"Then, if a certain girl detective is willing to chaperone a ride to the park, I'll inform him that I know he's my admirer and of the schoolboard's new ruling. After all, since I heard he is going to open a newspaper office here in Redemption, I think we would make a good match, the schoolteacher and the newsman. If he has any inclination to court me, I believe that will leave an opening for him to ask Papa Bart if he can."

"I can't see why he wouldn't accept or ask; he's gone to a lot of trouble to get your attention. Will you inform him that you know he's your secret admirer?"

"Oh yes. I plan to do that when I invite him to dinner tomorrow. Hopefully, he'll own up to it so this whole thing can be turned into something positive, and maybe I'll end up with a husband before long."

Their conversation turned to the rest of the school year and Levi's impending move east. Jayna couldn't help but think of the handsome man who had been leaving her gifts. She hoped he was willing to admit he was her admirer and agree to court her. She honestly would love to become Mrs. Thaddeus Richmond, but it would be up to him to own up to being her admirer and asking to court her.

If he did or didn't, she would move forward on finding other things she could do to help Cindy achieve her goal of becoming a Lady Pinkerton agent. She started thinking of ways to direct a part of Cindy's schoolwork toward helping her young friend prepare for her dream be fulfilled. After all, she could think of no better career for Cindy Ryder, the girl detective.

About the Author

George McVey always wanted to be a superhero; sadly, no radioactive storms or animals have been a part of his life. One day while spinning a tall tale for his family, someone suggested once again that with all his experiences in ministry, and his imagination, he should be writing books. This time it was like lightning struck him and he decided, why not.

Since then, George has been hard at work using his creative imagination and writing several books. He's still adding to his bibliography to this day. You can find them all on his Amazon.com page https://www.amazon.com/-/e/B007E39QUG.

George lives in the wonderful state of Almost Heaven, West Virginia, in a lovely creekside trailer with his wife of 33 years, Sheri, and a service dog named Daisy Mae.

If you ever come to visit him, you will probably find him sitting in his recliner or at his desk in the office working on some writing project. If he isn't working on a novel, he will be working on a short story or blog post. If he isn't doing either of those, then he is either asleep or eating, his other two favorite pastimes.

You can reach him by email at pastor.george.mcvey@gmail.com. You can also find out more about his books, get a free book, or join his beta readers team to help make the books he sells better at his website http://georgemcvey.weebly.com. You can also connect with George on Facebook at his readers group. George's Gorgeous Readers. https://www.facebook.com/groups/858552084327160

Books by George

You can find all of George's books on his Amazon author page.
https://www.amazon.com/-/e/B007E39QUG.